This book is dedicated to
Flozzy Slippin because I never got
her anything for her birthday.

x X x

 SOUTH

D0544272
S

EGMONT

We bring stories to life

First published in paperback in Great Britain 2012
by Egmont UK Limited,
239 Kensington High Street, London W8 6SA

Text copyright © 2012 Kjartan Poskitt
Illustrations copyright © 2012 David Tazzyman

The moral rights of the author and illustrator have been asserted

ISBN 978 1 4052 5777 0

1 3 5 7 9 10 8 6 4 2

www.egmont.co.uk

A CIP catalogue record for this title is available from the British Library

Printed and bound by CPI Group (UK) Ltd, Croydon, CR0 4YY

All rights reserved. No part of this publication may be reproduced,
stored in a retrieval system, or transmitted, in any form or by any means,
electronic, mechanical, photocopying, recording or otherwise,
without the prior permission of the publisher and copyright owner.

48134/1

EGMONT LUCKY COIN

Our story began over a century ago, when seventeen-year-old
Egmont Harald Petersen found a coin in the street.

He was on his way to buy a flyswatter, a small hand-operated
printing machine that he then set up in his tiny apartment.

The coin brought him such good luck that today Egmont has
offices in over 30 countries around the world. And that lucky
coin is still kept at the company's head offices in Denmark.

Agatha Parrot

and the Mushroom Boy

Typed out neatly by
Kjartan Poskitt

Illustrated by David Tazzyman

EGMONT

The gang!

Bianca can do hippopotamus impressions on her trombone. Ha ha wicked!

Warning! **Martha**'s mouth is like a bucket with teeth. If she's hungry ... keep back!

Agatha (that's me). The last time I had my hair cut, the lady found a snail. And that's true.

Ivy's new skateboard only lasted 23 seconds. No brakes. No steering. It was awesome.

Ellie still has her fairy outfit just in case they ever come into fashion.

Odd Street
Primary
School

ODD STREET

No 1
Bianca

No 3
Martha

No 5
Agatha

No 7
Ivy

No 9
Ellie

SCHOOL

HELPFUL TIP

When you get to the word
COO-EE you're exactly halfway
through the book. So if you want
to save the second half of the book
for later that's where to stop.

CONTENTS

What is the Point of Big Brothers?

. . . .

Before we start, have you got a big brother? If you do then you're going to LOVE this book.

1

Even if you don't have one, I bet you'll be nodding as you read it saying to yourself, 'Well done Agatha, wahoo! Go for it girl . . .' especially right at the end when James gets turned into a mushroom. Oh, sorry about that, that's supposed to be the surprise ending. You'll have to forget the mushroom bit now until you get to it.

(Gosh, I just had a thought — you might actually be a big brother yourself. But if you are I bet you're really cool and always offer your sweets round and never hog the computer to play stupid video games. So this book isn't at all about you! I promise promise promise it isn't, so keep reading.)

Anyway, my name is Agatha Jane Parrot and thanks for reading this book! As you might have guessed I HAVE got a big brother who's called James. He gets called some other things too but the old bloke who is typing this story out for me says we're not allowed to put words like that in a book or you wouldn't be allowed to read it ha ha!

It's very hard to think of anything good about having a big brother, and if you don't believe me then ask the QUEEN. If she had a big brother then she wouldn't be queen, because he would get to be

king instead, even if she was really nice and he was totally horrible. The big brother king could choose which bedroom he wanted in the palace and he'd get all the best jobs like launching ships and going to see brand new films. Even at dinner time they'd never take turns as to who gets the sauce first, it would always be him.

I bet the Queen would be desperate to turn her big brother

into a mushroom because then he'd be King Mushroom the First ha ha! (Sorry, I didn't mean to remind you about the mushroom bit so you'll just have to forget it again.)

Of course nobody minds having LITTLE brothers. My friend Ellie Slippin at number 9 has two twin ones and they're dead funny because like all little kids their heads are a bit too big for their bodies so when they run they can't do corners very fast and they end up banging into the wall BAM! Later on in the story there's a bit where the twins both bang their heads on a bucket which is dead funny too but we haven't got there yet.

Unfortunately for me, James isn't the little funny type of brother, he's the big smelly evil type. Just to prove it, here's a list of evil things he did last week with marks out of ten for evilnessity:

MONDAY: He came in from football all muddy and then sat on MY bed and then Mum blamed ME for it (6/10).

TUESDAY: He grabbed my

packet of crisps and scrunched them up into mush before I could eat them (4/10).

WEDNESDAY: When we were getting ready to go to school he stood outside the bathroom and twiddled the door handle all the time when I was inside which put me off doing anything and I ended up having to go out of class in the middle of quiet reading time and Ivy Malting who sits next to me held her breath all the time I was away which made everybody laugh when I came back because she was blue in the cheeks and rolling about which I admit was pretty funny so we love Ivy **WAHOO GO IVY** but we do NOT love James (9/10).

THURSDAY: He spent all day just generally being a boy (2/10). (Actually he does this every day, but I know he can't help it so I only gave him 2/10.)

FRIDAY: He finished off the lemonade without asking, and then he did a big burp right in my face (7/10).

Of course this is the sort of thing that everybody with a big brother has to put up with, but when it got to Saturday James did his most evil crime EVER. (It has to score 11/10 at least.)

Before you look at the next chapter to read about it, don't forget that you have to forget about James getting turned into a mushroom or it'll ruin the end for you. Have you forgotten it? Not thinking about boys being turned into mushrooms? No? Good. Off we go then . . .

The Start

• •

For me, seven o'clock on Saturday evenings can only mean one thing . . .

Sing, Wiggle and Shine!

It is absolutely the second best programme on the telly.

Of course I never get to watch

the FIRST BEST programme because that's *Celebrities at the Dentist* and Mum always comes in and says, 'I will NOT have you watching that rubbish,' then she turns it off and sends me upstairs and THEN she puts it straight back on and curls up watching it with a box of chocolates.

Oh well. When I'm a mum I'm not going to have kids. I'm going to get on with my own life and not go bothering other people just because they're younger than me.

Sing, Wiggle and Shine is for
unfamous people who want to be

famous. I'd watched every show in the series for the whole 26 weeks and at last – *da-daddle-ah-da-da-daaaah* – they'd got to the final! Along the way they'd kicked off about 200 losers including the bloke with the rabbit ears who hopped around singing *Carrots Are a Bunny's Best Friend*, oh he was just so brilliant I wish they'd do t-shirts of him.

Anyway, there I was sitting on the sofa and the last three people had just finished singing, wiggling and shining. I really wanted Sophie to win because Lauren had stupid earrings and Darren had his hairy chest showing which is hardly suitable for family viewing is it? It looked like he had a doormat stuffed up his shirt. Yuk. And anyway I felt sorry for Sophie because her shoe flew off in the dancing bit and then she forgot her words, and then she cried when she told everybody how

poorly her hamster was so COME
ON SOPHIE. Eeeek . . . it was all
too exciting!

The judges had got together
in their very last judges' huddle.
That's when they all put their heads
together and whisper so it's a good
job my friend Ellie's not a judge as
she's always got nits and they'd all
end up scratching ha ha!

'And now we come to the big
exciting moment!' said Grin Sickly.

He's the presenter whose hair looks like a mouldy cycle helmet. Oh gosh I was so wound up I was biting the sofa cushion. 'Tonight's winner will become a huge international star! And to tell us who it is, will you please welcome last year's winner . . .'

BIG APPLAUSE.

'Oh, sorry. He'll be here in a minute, he's still locking his bike and changing out of his overalls.'

CLICK! That's when the telly

switched channel.

Evil big brother James had sneaked into the living room, grabbed the remote control and then plonked himself in the armchair.

'Turn that back!' I shouted.

'No way,' he said. 'The football's on in five minutes.'

'But they're just about to announce the winner.'

'Tough. You've been watching for ages. My turn.'

Before I knew it, I'd thrown myself at James to get the remote off him but YUK he shoved it under his bottom and sat on it. I tried to drag him off the chair, but he was grabbing on to the arms too tightly.

'Please James, turn it back. PLEASE!'

'No way,' said James. 'It's the adverts. Football's on straight after the adverts. Besides I like the adverts.'

You see what I mean about big

brothers? Evil evil evil. And selfish. The only chance I had was to run into the kitchen to get Dad. He was baking one of his monster cakes for our school fete **Guess the Weight of the Cake** competition. There was a big baking tin full of sloppy cake mix in the middle of the table, and he was at the sink washing out the mixing bowl.

'Don't tell me,' said Dad. 'I know, I heard.'

'Then make him give the remote back,' I said.

'James!' Dad shouted. 'Let her see the results, then you can turn it back.'

I could hear the TV saying what fun it is to have car insurance.

'He's not turning it over Dad,' I said. 'It'll be too late now.'

'JAMES. Turn it over.'

But the TV just went on to talk about a sort of shampoo that makes men give flowers to ladies.

'JAMES,' shouted Dad. 'You can watch football in two minutes IF Agatha can watch her programme NOW. Otherwise I'll empty my ELECTRIC SHAVER out all over your pillow and you'll scratch yourself to DEATH in your sleep tonight. And I mean it.'

The TV went off then James shouted through from the living room, 'Here then you BIG BABY.'

Without looking he hurled the remote

in through the kitchen door.

OW! It cracked me right on the

head.

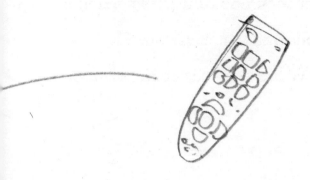

Dad was so busy admiring how shiny the mixing bowl was that he didn't see what happened and so I didn't bother telling him. He'd only have

27

come up with one of his silly made-up punishments. And besides, I knew I'd missed the end of the programme.

Thunk thunk thunk . . . creak . . .

SLAM!

James had run upstairs and shut himself in his bedroom. How pathetic. He should have known that he can run but he can't hide from Agatha. He knew that he'd been a bully with the remote and therefore he was going to suffer. Oh yes he was indeed. *Sounds of dramatic music: Dah-dah-dahhhhh!*

(Read that last bit again out loud. Oh go on, don't be a wimp, you know you want to. This is the bit I mean:

Sounds of dramatic music: Dah-dah-dahhhhh!

If you're in your classroom having quiet reading time and you just did that nice and LOUD then you're awesome. Wahoo! Right, on with the next chapter, although the time has only moved forwards by about twenty seconds . . .)

Twenty Seconds
Later

. . . .

I was in the living room pulling all the cushions off the sofa and the armchairs. The idea was to make Dad come in and ask me what the matter was but he didn't, so I had to make some sad little sighing

31

noises too. Dad still didn't come in, so I had to make the sad little sighing noises louder and louder until they sounded like this: HOOOOOO-NAH. Yes I know that sounds more like a hippopotamus but at least it worked because at last Dad stuck his head in through the doorway.

'What's going on?' he said. 'I thought you wanted to watch your programme.'

'I do,' I said all sweet and innocent. 'But I don't know where James has hidden the remote. Oh well . . .' *dejected sigh* '. . . it'll all be finished now. I'll just have to watch the repeat on Monday. Or the backstage special on Tuesday or the highlights programme on Friday.'

Dad started picking up the cushions, feeling them for remote control-sized bumps, and then chucking them back. 'It's no good,' he said. 'I want to watch the film later. Where is that remote? James? JAMES?'

Upstairs James's bedroom door creaked open, and soon he was back down in the living room getting a good grilling. 'I passed it to Agatha,' he protested.

'But I was in the kitchen,' I said. 'How could you pass it to me unless you had the longest arms in the world?'

James was not looking happy at all.

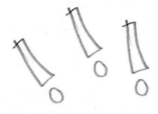

'Well, I sort of passed it,' he said. 'It'll be in there somewhere.'

'Then get it now please,' said Dad, and then he sat down in the armchair and opened his newspaper in front of his face in a daddish sort of way.

James went into the kitchen. He looked along the worktop, he looked under the table. Tee hee, no chance! He opened the fridge and looked inside, then he got the lid

off the rubbish bin and poked around in that. Ha ha ha! Of course I was only having a secret inside-my-head laugh. All James could see was me standing by the door looking serious.

'What did you do with it?' he demanded.

'You mean the remote? Don't ask me. You're the one who had it.'

'You should have caught it,' snapped James crossly. Oh deary me, the pressure was getting to him.

'Caught it?' I gasped in astonishment. 'You mean you *threw* it? Then maybe it went in the sink.'

'I hardly threw it at all,' said James nervously, but all the same he went to look. The sink was full of sticky cloudy water so he pulled the plug out and gradually it drained away. Yuk! There was just one teaspoon lying in the bottom. For a moment James looked happy, because he knew he'd have been in real trouble if the remote had landed in the water. It might have short-circuited and zapped itself to bits ha ha!

James was looking round blankly again. *Come on James*, I thought to myself. *Get that little baked-bean brain of yours going and THINK! Where is the very worst place that remote could have landed? Even worse than the sink?*

It was no good, he was never going to manage to work it out for himself so I had to give him a clue. I took a long deep sniff . . .

'Hmmm, that cake smells really nice Dad,' I said. 'How long before it comes out of the oven?'

'It'll be a few minutes yet,' said Dad's newspaper.

If James's head had been a giant light bulb it would have suddenly come on – **Ping!**

He spun round to stare at the oven and whispered to me: 'When did Dad put the cake in?'

'About the same time as you were stomping upstairs. Why?'

'Oh no!' His lip was trembling. 'And before that, was the cake mixture just sitting on the table?'

'Of course it was,' I said, keeping it innocent. 'Where else would it be?'

'So the remote must have landed

in the mixture, and now it's in the
. . . in the . . .'

'In the what, James?'

But of course he didn't need to
answer. He was staring at the oven
so hard that his eyes were almost out
 of his head HA HA HA!

My work was done. It was time
for Agatha to casually walk out of
the kitchen. Tumty tum. Tee tum-
tum. Tum.

Next Door
or Next Door to
Next Door

• •

The good thing about living at number 5 Odd Street is that all my best friends are either next door or next door to next door.

I desperately HAD to know who'd won *Sing, Wiggle and Shine*,

45

so while the cake was baking I went round to number 7 and rang the bell. There was a big noise like thunder **BAM BAM BAM** as mad Ivy came jumping down the stairs four at a time and then the door flew open. (That's the same Ivy as the Ivy who turned blue back on page 10.)

'It's AGATHA!' said Ivy and then she grabbed me and gave me a big hug as if she hadn't seen me for

a million years even though she sits

next to me at school all day.

'Hey Ivy,' I said. 'Did you see who won *Sing, Wiggle and Shine*?'

'When's it on?' asked Ivy.

'It's BEEN on,' I told her. 'Didn't you see it?'

'Aw no, I missed it,' said Ivy. 'Who won?'

So that was useless, so then me and Ivy went to number 9. Their doorbell is broken, but you don't need doorbells when you've got Ivy.

'Hey ELLIE!' shouted Ivy

through the letter box. 'Are you in there? Did you see *Sing, Wiggle and Shine*?'

The door opened and Ellie was there holding her tiny baby sister who is just SO cute. The baby was only wearing a nappy and was wrapped in an old sweatshirt. Her little toes sticking off the end of her feet looked just like Rice Krispies and she had the most brilliantly snotty nose.

'I had to give Bubbles a bath,' said Ellie proudly. 'She had jam stuck in her tummy button.'

'A jammy tummy button? Oh that's well cool!' said Ivy.

Bah. A jammy tummy button might be well cool but it didn't help me so next we went to number 1. Bianca opened the door holding her trombone and we asked her if she knew who'd won.

'Sorry, I was traying my plum

bone,' she said.

'Eh?' said me and Ivy.

'Like this,' said Bianca and then
blew a big blast **BWARB!**

'Oh!' we said. 'She was PLAYing
her TROMbone!'

We love Bianca. Don't always
understand her but love her.

The only door left to try was
number 3. Ivy got Bianca to point
her trombone at the letter box.
I held the flap open and Bianca

did a big **BWARB-WAB-WARRRRB** in through the hole ha ha wicked!

We could hear Martha laughing even before she opened the door because she's big and jolly and laughs at everything.

'Agatha! Perfect timing,' she said when she appeared. It was like she was expecting me. 'Here's that stuff your dad wanted to go on his cake.'

Martha held up a huge carrier bag from the shop her mum works at. It's called Spendless and everything they sell has funny wrappings and it's made by people you've never heard of. Martha opened it up to show us. 'There's icing, jam, chocolate sauce, crisps . . .'

'CRISPS? Honestly Martha you can't put crisps on a cake!'

'Why not?' asked Martha holding up a packet with strange writing on. 'They're pink so we think they're prawn cocktail flavour. They go with anything. Besides they're well past their use-by date so Mum put them in for free.'

'Free?' said Dad who had just stuck his head out of our front door which is next door. 'YUM! Do thank your mum for me.'

He reached over the fence, took the bag and went back in. Martha was about to go back in her house too but I stopped her.

'Did you see *Sing, Wiggle and Shine*?' I asked.

'Absolutely no way!' said Martha.

'We're watching the football.'

'But it's Rovers playing,' I said. 'You hate Rovers.'

'Too right I do,' grinned Martha. 'And they're losing three-nil. It's awesome!'

Martha hurried back inside her house. Ellie had already shut her door and Bianca did another **BWARB** and went back in too. That just left me and Ivy who was swinging on our gate.

'How come YOU didn't see the programme anyway?' asked Ivy. I told her all about the evilness of James. 'You can't let him get away with that!' she said.

I must have pulled a face or something because Ivy fell off the gate and banged her head on the fence in excitement. 'Oh WOW!' she blurted out. 'You've already done something haven't you? I know. I can tell.'

'No I haven't,' I said.

'Yes you have, yes you have, yes you have,' said Ivy. 'What what what?'

Honestly! We were standing right outside our house with the door open and James could have been listening. There was no way I was going to tell Mrs Big Mouth Ivy anything.

'Tell me the truth or I'll HATE you,' said Ivy.

So Ivy just had to go back into her own house and hate me. I can be dead tough like that.

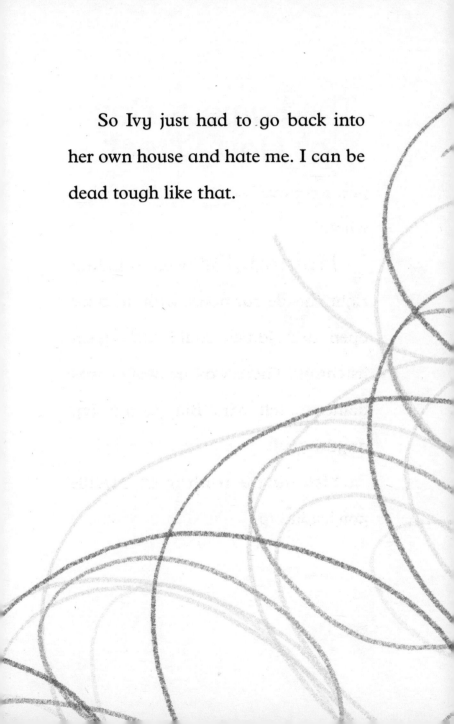

The Famous Cake of Odd Street

. . . .

When I got back into the kitchen, the cake was out of the oven and cooling on the table. Dad was digging through Martha's bag of stuff, but then he looked up and caught James almost sticking his face in the cake and prodding it

62

with his finger.

'James!' said Dad. The Guilty
Boy jumped backwards so hard that
he crashed into the fridge. 'Will you
stop poking and wiping your nose on
that cake? People are going to eat it.'

Dad opened up the bag and lifted
out a massive block of bright yellow
icing that almost hurt your eyes to
look at. 'What do you think of this,
then?' he asked proudly. 'It was on
special offer.'

I bet it was. I think I'd rather eat the bit of cake that James wiped his nose on, but Dad can never resist anything on special offer. He tipped all the other special offers out of the bag. There was about three tonnes of coloured sprinkles, squirty toppings, sweets, chocolate shapes and of course some dodgy pink crisps. Yahoo, good old Dad! If you're making a cake for a Guess the Weight of the Cake competition, you don't want it to look boring.

Dad and me began rolling out the icing and slapping it on the cake, but James just stood in the corner having a bit of a panic.

'Do you want to do a bit, James?' I asked him nicely like the lovely sister I am.

'I'd rather he found that remote,' said Dad as he aimed a strawberry sauce squirter at the cake. 'Because

James isn't going to get any pocket money till it turns up.'

BLOSH!
SPLUDGE!
SQUIRTY PLOP!

We'd been decorating the cake for about half an hour, and the yellow icing was completely covered with flowers, stars, hearts, rockets and a rather lovely skull. The whole soggy lump was dripping with so much strawberry and chocolate topping

that it had run off all over the table. There were just a few tiny silver sugar balls left on a saucer.

'Shall I put these on Dad?' I asked.

'Hmmm . . .' he said having a deep artistic contemplation to himself. 'Nah, better not. We don't want to overdo it.'

Just then we heard the front door open. 'We're home!' shouted Mum and then little sister Tilly ran in wearing her ballet skirt.

'What's that?' said Tilly when she saw the cake.

'It's for the school fete on Monday,' I told her.

'Oh,' said Tilly wrinkling her nose.

'Do you like it?' asked Dad proudly.

That was a mistake. You should never ask Tilly if she likes anything, because you always get the same answer.

'Hmmm . . . bit boring,' said Tilly, then she ran upstairs to get changed.

'She's wrong,' said Dad sounding hurt. 'This cake is a legend. In years to come there'll be coach tours going down Odd Street showing people where it was made. It's one of the all-time greats.' He took some photos of the cake on his phone then wrapped a big sheet of cling film round it. Finally he took one more photo and then went upstairs for a bath because he was covered in yellow icing, flour, cream and squirty toppings. James was still staring at the cake like it was about to bite him.

'What is your problem?' I asked.

'The TV remote's in there,' whispered James. 'It has to be!' He went to the kitchen drawer and got a long metal meat spike out. 'I'll see if I can feel it.' James was just about to stick the spike into the top of the cake.

'Are you mad?' I warned him. 'Dad will go nuts if you burst the cling film.'

'Then how can I find out? I have to know!'

BBC2 is a
Chocolate Flower

• •

A few minutes later I was keeping watch by the living room door. James was standing in front of the telly which was quietly showing a cooking programme. He was clutching the wrapped cake and was gently prodding the top with his

72

finger. Suddenly the door opened and James spun round, almost dropping the cake.

'Relax,' I told him. 'It's only Tilly.'

'What's James doing?' asked Tilly.

'He's trying to see if he can change the telly channel using the cake,' I said.

'That's a bit boring,' said Tilly. 'Why doesn't he use the remote?'

'Don't tell her I lost it!' James snapped bossily. He kept prodding the cake, trying to push as hard as he dared without messing up the fancy patterns. He was just about to give up when the telly suddenly

74

boomed out:

'. . . *AND THE PUDDING IS CALLED CHOCOLATE SURPRISE BECAUSE* . . .'

'Argh!' cried James, stabbing at the cake even harder. 'I must have hit the volume button. Shhh! Please shhh . . . !'

'. . . *WHEN YOU DIG YOUR SPOON IN, YOU FIND* . . . *TWO PAIRS OF TROUSERS AND AN OLD WELLINGTON*

*BOOT AND . . . NOTTINGHAM
RAILWAY STATION.'*

'Now it's changing channels,'
said James. 'The chocolate flower is
BBC2 and the green star is Channel
5. The remote is definitely in here!'

'What did James say?' shouted
Tilly, trying to make herself heard
over the telly. Before she got an
answer, we heard Mum shouting
from the top of the stairs.

'Why is that telly on so loud?'

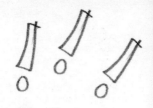

'James, she's coming!' I warned him. 'Try pressing the red Smartie.' So James pressed the red Smartie and to his relief the telly got quieter.*

(*You'll find out how I knew the telly would get quieter later on. It's a bit of excitement I'm saving up for you. And anyway it's unfair if I tell you now when I didn't tell Ivy.)

By the time Mum came into the room, the cake was back on the kitchen table and we were all sitting watching an old man with a big nose talking about train timetables.

'What programme's this?' asked Mum suspiciously.

'It's something James wanted to watch,' I told her. 'Isn't it James?'

'It's a bit boring,' said Tilly.

Mum knew something was going on, but as the house didn't seem to be falling down, she hadn't the energy to care.

'Tilly, you get a quick drink and

then up to bed,' she said. 'And you two, keep that telly quiet.'

A few minutes later James was in the kitchen having a panic. Tilly had gone upstairs to do her teeth, and we could hear Mum walking around the main bedroom telling Dad off for getting chocolate on the carpet.

'Maybe we could make a list of what sweets to press on the cake to

change the telly,' said James. 'Then Dad could use it and stop worrying about the remote. We'll just say the cake is magic or something.'

'So you're expecting dad to sit there every night with that cake on his knee, poking it with his finger?' I asked. James nodded. Honestly, he's such a loser! 'Forget it. We have to take that cake to the school fete tomorrow.'

'But I have to get the remote out,'

said James. 'And if I cut the cake up Dad will kill me.'

'He couldn't kill you if it was yours,' I said. James looked puzzled so I had to explain it a bit more. 'Suppose you actually won the cake tomorrow and brought it home, you could do what you liked with it.'

'Oh very funny,' said James. 'How am I supposed to guess the weight?'

Well **DURRR!** There's only

a set of weighing scales in the kitchen cupboard isn't there? He could have put the cake on them . . . but as James didn't think of that, I suggested something really stupid instead.

'All you need to do is get the cake recipe and then add up all the different bits,' I said.

I was only joking, but before I knew it, James had pulled the tatty old cookbook off the shelf and found the right page. Ha ha!

'170 grams of flour, 170 grams of butter, 170 grams of sugar, three eggs . . .' he read.

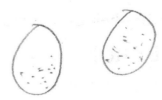

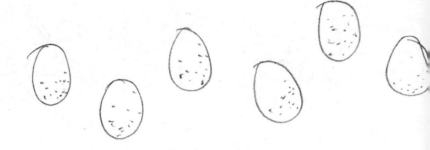

'Dad used six eggs,' I told him. 'So he must have used more than it says of everything.'

'So instead of three eggs it was six, so how much flour would that be . . .' James got out a pencil and paper. 'And how much does an egg weigh anyway?'

'Don't forget the icing,' I said helpfully. 'And the toppings.'

And then James did something that made me a bit jealous. He made a really loud sad little sighing noise and he didn't sound like a hippopotamus one bit. So it IS possible after all!

I left him in the kitchen scribbling away like mad. To be honest I was wondering if I was being too mean to him, but then again, my head still hurt where it got bashed by the remote, and thanks to him I still didn't know who'd won *Sing, Wiggle and Shine*. So no, Agatha, you were not being too mean. The boy James had asked for trouble, and he was getting it. Good.

The Lucky Guess

• •

It was after school on Monday and the playground was full of wobbly old tables with wobbly old teachers standing behind them. Me and Tilly and James had just met up with Mum and Dad by the school gates when . . .

88

'AGATHA AGATHA AGATHA!'

Ivy came charging over and grabbed my arm and spun me round a few times. She was a bit hyper because she'd had a biscuit from Martha's mum's tea stall, and it had got some of that same yellow icing on it that we'd put on the cake. There's something in those bright colours that makes Ivy turn into . . . well, Ivy really.

'COME ON!' she shouted and then went running off round the tables and shouting out what she thought of each one.

The first table Ivy looked at had Mrs Twelvetrees selling her raffle tickets ('WOW!' shouted Ivy). Next to her Miss Barking was selling organic cardigans that she'd

knitted from some weird stuff she grows on her allotment ('**WOW!**').

Then there was a chair where you could sit and have your toenails painted by Motley the caretaker (WOW   WOW   WOW

TOTALLY AWESOME WOW!'),

NEARLY NEW LIB-
RARY BOOKS

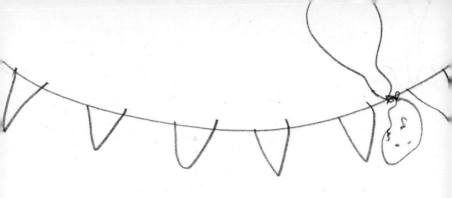

and just along from that, the school receptionist Miss Wizzit was selling 'nearly new' books which had been rescued when the library had got flooded, and they were still a bit squidgy ('**WOW!**').

ORANGE
SQUASH
10P

As you can see, the person who most impressed Judge Ivy was Motley, so he needs a big round of applause clap clap clap WOW.

'But that's silly,' said Mum. 'Who's going to be daft enough to get their toenails painted?'

Motley looked a bit hurt. 'I'll do you a special offer. How about six toes for the price of five?'

'Special offer?' said Dad. 'Ooooh...'

In the middle of everything was

a table with a small stool standing on it. The legs of the stool were wrapped in silver tin foil to make it look posh and groovy, and sitting proudly on top was Dad's cake. ('WOW! EH? WHAT? OH. WOW!' Thank you Ivy for that intelligent contribution.)

Pinned on the front of the stool was a smart little sign:

Guess the weight of the cake
20p

97

Guess the
weight of
the cake
20p

On the table beside it were some old weighing scales out of the school kitchen, and standing next to them was our class teacher Miss Pingle looking very serious. She's the one who keeps dyeing her hair different colours, and on Monday it was a rather fetching shade of police-trousers blue to make herself look more official.

Miss Pingle was in charge of taking the money and writing down

everybody's guesses. She was desperate to do a good job because she's a new teacher and normally she only gets to pour out the orange squash. (By the way, it had taken her eighteen goes just to print the sign out on the computer. Of course she didn't actually tell anybody that, but earlier on me and Martha had found numbers one to seventeen scrunched up in the recycling bin. You can't fool us ha ha!)

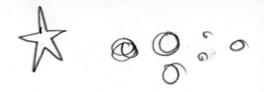

By now Ivy was starting to calm down a bit and had reached the stage where she had to hug somebody and the nearest somebody was me. It's quite nice for a short time, but you don't need too much of it. Luckily Bianca saw us and came over.

'Don't worry Agatha,' said Bianca. 'Ivy can bug me for a hit.'

Eh? But then Bianca took Ivy off me. She must have meant to say '*hug* me for a *bit*'. YO! Good one

Bianca. Top girl.

Meanwhile James had been standing over by the railings and watching a few people have a guess.

'675 grams,' said Ivy's mum.

James had a big grin on his face so I went to ask him why. 'That's way too small!' he told me.

Thank goodness for that. We didn't need Ivy's mum winning the cake. You've just seen what one little biscuit's worth of icing does for Ivy, so imagine what a whole cake would do. We'd be pulling her off the moon. Wahoo – GO IVY! We love Ivy.

'3,762 grams,' said Bianca's mum.

'Miles too big!' muttered James happily.

Then we saw Martha pulling an old gentlemen over to see Miss Pingle. 'This is my grandad,' said Martha. 'He used to be a baker so he'll know.'

'That cake will be about 43 ounces,' said Martha's grandad, handing over his 20p.

'We don't measure in ounces these days,' said Miss Pingle who wasn't really sure what an ounce was. 'We use grams.'

'Oh, righto,' smiled the jolly old gentleman who was admiring Miss Pingle's blue hair. 'Can you convert 43 ounces to grams for me?'

'Of course,' said Miss Pingle and

104

she carefully wrote down *43 grams.*★

(★Warning! The old bloke who is typing this book out says that ounces used to be the old-fashioned way of weighing things. What's more 43 ounces is not even close to being 43 grams, so if you say it is then you'll sound like a bit of a weirdo. Mind you, the old bloke says that the real answer is that 43 ounces = 1,219·03 grams. Gosh, anybody who knows that would have to be a

COMPLETE weirdo – just like he is! Ha ha ha . . . oh ok, I'm only kidding. Keep typing please.)

James was starting to feel confident. Nobody had come close to the number he'd worked out yet, but then Gwendoline Tutt marched over to the table. She's the one who lives at the top end of Odd Street in the big house with the tree in front and a space to park two cars. She hates school fetes, but her mum told

her that she had to have one go on
everything before she could leave.

'One two three four,' said
Gwendoline Tutt
slapping down
her 20p coin.

Her best friend Olivia Livid was with her and they both sniggered rudely.

'Do you mean one thousand, two hundred and thirty-four grams?' asked Miss Pingle.

'Yeah, whatever,' said Gwendoline. 'I don't want to win the stupid thing anyway.'

'It looks gross,' agreed Olivia and then the two of them walked off to make rude remarks about something else.

Next to me James slumped back against the railings like he'd been thumped by a ghost.

'Aren't you going to have your go?' I asked him.

'No point!' he groaned. 'I spent all night working out the exact weight of that cake, and then Gwendoline Tutt just guessed it. She'll win and she doesn't even want to.'

'Oh dear oh dear what a big pity,' I said being a lovely sister. 'But maybe you didn't get it exactly right? You could try guessing one gram more than Gwendoline, and then just to be sure, guess one gram less?'

'But that's two goes!' wailed James. 'That'll cost 40p.'

'It's either that or you'll get no more pocket money ever,' I reminded him. 'So quick, do it now before somebody else guesses those same numbers.'

James thought about it for a

moment, then hurried over to pay his 40p. Miss Pingle carefully wrote down *1233g – J Parrot* and also *1235g – J Parrot*.

'You seem very sure, James,' said Miss Pingle suspiciously. 'I hope you didn't weigh the cake at home before it got here?'

Ha ha ha ha! You should have seen James's face.

'Oh no, I'd never dream of doing that!' said James wishing he *had*

dreamed of it. It would have saved him a whole night of sitting up doing tricky sums. Poor little James.

Mean Old Mum and Martha's Milkshake

• •

After the first rush of wild excitement, there's always about an hour of school fetes which is really boring. That's because everybody has to hang around until Mrs Twelvetrees gives out the raffle

113

prizes, and she *never* does that until she's dead certain that we've all got tickets.

Most people are like Martha's mum who bought loads of tickets for Martha because she always does. Lucky Martha.

Unlucky me.

Our mum HATES buying raffle tickets and she makes it totally embarrassing. Usually she tries to sneak away early, but this time we

all had to wait for Dad's cake to be weighed, and that was going to be after the raffle. Thank goodness! If they'd weighed the cake before the raffle, it would have ruined my revenge on James as you'll see.

Mum was standing in the middle of the playground with Tilly swinging on her arm, and chatting away with some other mums (who all got tickets for themselves AND got tickets for their kids by the way).

Suddenly . . .

'I say, COO-EE! Mrs Parrot? HELLO!'

Mrs T cruised up alongside Mum, clutching a cake tin full of money. All the other mums laughed a bit and dived out of the way leaving our mum to face the Mighty Twelvetrees all by herself. Mum was already trying to be tough and pull her *no thank you* face, but it's not as if she had any choice about it. Headteachers are specially trained to hunt down mean old mums.

'I just wanted to say . . .' said Mrs T sadly, '. . . how jolly sorry I am that Tilly only got to say two words in the infants concert last week.'

'Pardon?' Mum was caught completely by surprise. 'Oh! It really doesn't matter . . .' she said feebly, trying to ignore the rolls of raffle tickets being waved right under her nose. Tilly was staring up at her crossly.

'I'm sure you'd want her to get

a few more lines next time, wouldn't you?' said Mrs Twelvetrees. Tilly started hopping up and down excitedly. Mrs T did her killer lipsticky smile. 'Tickets are five for a pound – *oh thank you!* – and who knows, maybe one day Tilly might get to sing a whole song . . .'

KUD-DINK. Before Mum even knew it, she'd dropped some money into the cake tin and Mrs T had whizzed off to trap her next victim.

'YOO-HOO! HELLO! I just wanted to say how jolly sorry I am that we didn't have space to include Henry in the lunchtime ping-pong group this term . . .'

Good for Mrs Twelvetrees. She needs to grab all the money she can to keep the staffroom emergency biscuit cupboard topped up or the teachers will start rioting. And that's true.

So anyway, Mum had bought a

121

measly five tickets. That meant it was one for her, one each for James, Tilly and Dad (wherever he'd got to) and **OH YIPPEE WHAT A TREAT** one whole ticket for me. It was number 610. **Whoopee.**

Once Mrs T had worked out that she'd hoovered up every single bit of spare cash in the place, she rang her handbell **CLANG DANG BLANG**. 'Action stations gang!' she called out. 'We'll weigh the cake in a minute, but first we'll draw the raffle. There's lots of super-dooper prizes so good luck everybody!'

'WOOO!' Everybody gave a big cheer for the super-dooper prizes.

Martha was getting all excited. She was desperate to win a great big green peppermint milkshake thing somebody had made up. YUK! But that's Martha for you. (The important thing is that the milkshake had a long stripy straw

sticking out of it which you've got to remember. It turns up later on.)

'Now then chaps,' said Mrs T. 'Who would like to come and pull some numbers out of the bucket and pass them to me?'

Ellie Slippin's little brothers immediately ran forwards and then couldn't stop so they both banged their heads on the bucket *donk donk!* They shoved their hands in and threw bundles of scrunched up

tickets at Mrs Twelvetrees. Gosh if me and Ivy had done that we'd be **DEAD**, but a couple of the dads started laughing, so the Slippin twins went on to have a full-on ticket snowball fight which was brilliant, especially when all the other little tiddly tots joined in.

I expect headteachers are supposed to get a bit ratty when this happens, but Mrs Twelvetrees had her cake tin full of dosh so she was too happy to care. She just picked a few tickets out of the kids' hair and shouted out the numbers.

Soon the playground was rocking to the sound of parents cheering and whooping as they won super-dooper prizes like a tin of peas or a little basket of fizzy bath salts. Tilly charged to the front when she heard her number, and came back proudly clutching a bag of instant cat food. Shame we haven't got a cat. Well, not one that's still alive anyway.

Eventually the only thing left was the peppermint milkshake, and about the only person still paying any attention was Martha. Mrs T held up one last ticket.

'And finally number 19,' she said.

Martha looked really sad. She hadn't got number 19, but nobody else was claiming the milkshake either.

'We can't wait all day!' said Mrs T. 'I'll pick another . . .'

'Wait,' I shouted. **'It's ME!'**

I went up, showed my ticket and came back with the glass of green gunk.

'You're soooo lucky!' sulked Martha.

'Don't be like that,' I said. 'I got it for you.'

'Oh **WOW** thanks, are you sure?' gasped Martha, but

she'd already grabbed it in case I changed my mind. She shoved the straw in her mouth and was about to take a slurp but then she stopped. 'Hang on . . . the number was 19. Your ticket was 610!'

'Hmmm, yes . . . technically it was. But if you show 610 to somebody quickly, and it's upside down with your thumb over the zero . . .'

SLURRRRP! went

Martha who was already not

listening.

The Silver Bullet

· ·

When the raffle was finished, Mrs Twelvetrees moved over to the cake. 'Oh by golly, hasn't Mr Parrot made us a super cake?' she said. 'Is he here?'

I'm not sure how she missed him actually as Dad was hopping

around over by Motley clutching his shoes and socks and waiting for his toenails to dry. Instead Mrs T spotted us and did that big lipsticky smile which made Mum instinctively grab a tight hold of her purse. But Mrs T only wanted to ask what flavour it was.

'I haven't the *remote*-est idea,' I said giving James a big poke in the ribs and he went bright red ha ha!

Miss Pingle lifted the cake down

off the stool and put it on one side of the scales. They were the old-fashioned sort of balance scales like a see-saw where you put what you're weighing on one side and then put different weights on the other side until it balances. Miss Pingle opened a smart little box. In it was a set of shiny weights of different sizes and all looking very important. First she took out some of the biggest weights and put them on the scales one at a time. 'That's a thousand grams, now I'm adding an extra hundred . . . and now another hundred . . .'

So far that made 1,200 grams which was getting to be a lot, but it still wasn't enough to make the scales move and lift the cake up.

'I'll put some smaller weights on now,' said Miss Pingle. She added a twenty and a ten, and then the cake just started to twitch.

'Ooooh!' said everybody.

'Ladies and gentlemen,' announced Miss Pingle seriously. 'We've got to 1,230 grams so now I'll go up one gram at a time until the cake balances.'

'How jolly super!' said Mrs Twelvetrees.

James was getting really excited. He had guessed 1,233 and 1,235 so he was still in with a good chance. Gwendoline and Olivia were over by the railings trying to look bored. But then I noticed a little huddle of heads all anxiously looking towards the scales. It was the whole Slippin family – mum, Ellie, her little sister Flozzy, the twins – all staring with their mouths wide open. Even baby Bubbles was staring out of her

battered old pushchair and dribbling all over her purple tights.

Behind me was a noise like a duck coughing. It was Martha slurping the last few drops of green milky sludge up through the long stripy straw. 'Hey Agatha,' she said laughing. 'Do you think my grandad gets a prize for the worst guess?'

'Never mind him,' I said. 'Ellie's family is looking a bit desperate!'

'Yeah, they really want to win,'

said Martha. 'It's Flozzy's birthday this week and they'd love to have that cake. They haven't got enough money to buy one that big in the shop.'

Oh dear. To be fair to James he had bought two tickets, and he'd spent hours working out how much the cake weighed so I'd sort of forgiven him and was hoping he'd win it. In fact anyone winning would be better than Gwendoline. But Ellie's family was looking so hopeful!

Cake weights:

1233 – J Parrot

1234 – G Tutt

1235 – J Parrot

1236 – F Slippin

I'd been watching the cake stand and I saw Flozzy Slippin's name was next to number 1236. It was going to be very close! All we could do was wait and see what happened.

Miss Pingle had got some tiny tweezers and was using them to pick

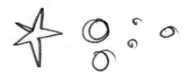

the very smallest weights out of the box. 'These are one gram weights,' she explained. 'I'll put them on one at a time until it balances.'

'Come on chaps, let's all count together,' said Mrs Twelvetrees.

'One!' said everybody as the first tiny weight went on. 'Two . . . three . . . oooh!'

The cake shifted ever so slightly. The weight had got to 1,233 grams which was one of James's guesses!

He had his fingers crossed so tightly that the ends were going blue . . . but the cake stayed where it was.

'Here comes weight number four,' announced Miss Pingle.

That would make a weight of 1,234 grams. Gwendoline and Olivia suddenly barged through everybody and pushed right to the front.

'You might win it,' said Olivia.

'I do hope not!' said Gwendoline. 'Can you imagine what Mum would say if I brought that thing home? It'd serve her right for making me come here.'

But Miss Pingle had already put the tiny weight on, and the cake stayed down.

'Well thank GOODNESS for that!' said Gwendoline. 'At least it won't be me that's poisoned.'

Gwendoline and Olivia pushed their way back to stand by the railings like they didn't care, but we all knew that Gwendoline was sulking her head off ha ha ha saddo!

'Let's add one more gram, Miss Pingle,' said Mrs Twelvetrees.

'Oooooh!' said the crowd.

James's crossed fingers went even bluer, and the Slippins's mouths all opened even wider and Bubbles's tights got even dribblier.

Very carefully, Miss Pingle tweezered the fifth tiny weight on to the scales. Everybody held their breath and then . . . the cake slowly rose up into the balanced position!

'YES!' screamed James. He was jumping up and down, punching the air. 'YES OH YES OH YES!'

'Who had 1,235 grams?' asked Miss Pingle looking round as if she couldn't see him. (Wasn't that a nice touch? She might only be a new teacher but she's got a lot of style.)

Everybody was looking at James, except me and Martha.

We were looking at the Slippins.

'That's really sad,' said Martha. 'I wanted them to win.'

Ellie's mum was fumbling in her pocket and pulled out a crumpled £5 note. She came over to James.

'Well done James,' she said. 'But if you don't want the cake, can I buy it off you? Please?'

James looked at the £5 note and pulled a face. 'You can't afford it.'

Ellie's mum sighed, but then Ellie

shoved her hand in her cardigan pocket and pulled out all the money she had. It was only a few coins, probably about 25p. She passed them to her mum who offered them to James along with the £5.

'You're kidding, aren't you?' sneered James. 'I tell you what. Give me £100 and it's yours.'

Oooh, I was getting cross and at first I didn't notice that Martha was tapping me on the arm. 'You're pulling your hair!' she said.

Too right I was. It's what I always do to wake my brain up. NO WAY could I let James have that cake now, but how could I fix it . . . ?

And then I felt something between my fingers, something very small, hard and round that had got stuck in my hair. I tugged it out.

It was a tiny silver ball! It must have landed there on Saturday when we'd been slapping all the icing and other stuff on the cake. Oh wow. All I had to do was drop the ball on to the cake to make it that tiny bit heavier and James would lose!

But Martha had been reading my mind. She pointed at James who was already pushing his way to the front. There was no way I could get to the cake before he did. *Eeky freak!*

James could have just picked up the cake and walked away, but of course, being James, he couldn't resist turning to the crowd and doing a big bow. Absolutely nobody clapped, but he didn't care. He just waved over at Ellie and her mum and shouted, 'I'll save you a few crumbs!'

Just as James was making me feel utterly sick, I felt Martha's fingers reaching into my hand. She grabbed the little silver ball and shoved it

in one end of the long stripy straw.
(See? I told you that straw was
important.) She took a deep breath,
put the other end in her mouth,
aimed it at the cake and **BLEW!**

The ball shot out and stuck itself deep into the yellow icing. James was doing one last bow when behind his back, the cake slowly went down and the weights came up again. YO! GOOD ONE MARTHA. I mean to say, honestly, how cool was that? We love Martha.

'I say chaps!' said Mrs Twelvetrees clapping her hands loudly. 'It looks like we're not quite there yet. Let's have another gram please Miss Pingle!'

And sure enough, one more gram went on and the cake moved back up into the balanced position.

'I declare the official weight as being one thousand, two hundred and thirty-six grams!' said Miss Pingle.

'WHAT?' blurted James who couldn't believe it.

'And that's the *final* result,' said Miss Pingle sharply.

And with that she heaved the cake from the scales and walked over to the Slippins who were all standing with their hands outstretched to take it. And this time everybody DID clap.

Well actually, everybody clapped except James.

Nasty Surprises

. . . .

That night Dad was sitting in the armchair trying to watch a programme about cars he couldn't afford to buy. Dad is one of those dads who can't watch telly unless he's holding the remote control, so he was being really grumpy. Mum had taken

Tilly out to ballet so there was only me and James in the house and James had gone to hide up in his room. That left me to face the great grumpiness of Dad alone so that wasn't very fair, was it? Never mind, I'd soon have it sorted out. Tum tee tum . . .

'Would you like me to sit on the floor by the telly and change it when you want, Dad?' I asked.

'Don't be silly,' said Dad, but then he had a think about it just like

I knew he would. 'If anybody should be doing that it should be James.'

Correct. Well done Dad. So let's get it organised shall we?

'I don't mind doing it, honestly, really,' said good little Agatha who wouldn't hurt a sausage. 'After all James is busy upstairs doing his homework.★ You can't ask him to sit there changing the telly.'

'Oh can't I?'

(★Big joke. All James ever does

156

in his room is put on his football shirt and look at himself in the mirror, and Dad knew it.)

And so it came to pass that one minute later James was sitting on the floor by the telly looking even grumpier than Dad ha ha!

'Make it a bit quieter,' Dad said. James reached for the buttons and turned the volume down.

'Have I got to stay here all night?' he moaned.

'Unless you go and get that remote,' said Dad. 'I paid for the telly, that was MY remote control,

you lost it, so until you find it, you ARE the remote control. Now stop talking and make it a bit louder.'

James sighed and reached for the buttons again.

The car programme finished so Dad made James flick through all the other channels. He only watched about ten seconds of each one and made James change the volume every time. Gosh Dad was being super-grumpy that night, which is a bit worrying for a grown man with rainbow-coloured toenails.

I was on the sofa pretending to read a book about something but I can't remember what as it was dead boring. Oh gosh, I shouldn't say that when YOU'RE reading this book should I? It might put you off reading books. OK, the book was about bananas and it was really interesting. Really, honest it was. You don't believe me do you? Bah. I'd better start this bit again. (Don't worry, you won't have to read this, they always cross these bits out before they send books to the printers.)

I was on the sofa just being on the

sofa and not doing anything special. So that wasn't really worth telling you was it? Anyway THE POINT I'M TRYING TO MAKE IS . . . even though James being on the floor was funny at first, I was starting to feel a bit sorry for him.

Of course he's a big brother and therefore he is evil and selfish, but I'm sure he hadn't meant to be so mean to Ellie's mum. He'd just got a bit excited when he thought he'd won the cake. In fact, if I'm being honest, sometimes he isn't mean at all.

I'll tell you a secret story that I hope nobody else remembers except me. One time when I was six, Ivy accidentally knocked my chocolate biscuit down the drain in the school playground and I cried for ages until James came over and gave me his. I bet it was just a dirty trick so that in future years I could never *completely* hate him, but even so, it's a trick that's worked. So, because of that chocolate biscuit, I was just deciding to help James out when . . . a little twinkly fairy skipped into the room.

Actually it wasn't a real fairy, it was Tilly wearing her glittery ballet dress and waving a silver wand. I used to have a dress like that and dead cool I looked too. In fact if I wasn't going to be a celebrity actress supermodel when I grow up, I think being a real fairy would be neat. The world needs more fairies flying round, doing magic and making sure that your apple hasn't got a brown mushy bit and that there's no sticky patch on the park bench when you want to sit down and useful stuff like that.

But James is a boy and so he has no magic in his heart. Instead he gave Tilly a dirty look and demanded: 'What DO you look like?'

'She's a beautiful fairy,' said Dad.

'Ping pang pell, magic spell,' said Tilly dancing around James. 'James's head is a big smelly potato.'

'Oh grow up!' snapped James. He grabbed Tilly's wand, bent it in half and threw it across the room. As Tilly burst into tears he shouted: 'I hate little sisters. Why can't you be a boy like normal people?'

Oh dear. And to think I'd been feeling sorry for him . . . well that hadn't lasted long! It was going to take more than a chocolate biscuit in the playground to save him now.

I found Tilly's wand and straightened it up for her, then Mum came in holding a little sparkly

white crown. 'Look Tilly, I found it,' she said putting it on Tilly's head. 'There everybody, do you like Tilly's costume? Flozzy Slippin is having a magic woodland party tomorrow, and Tilly's been invited.'

'How sad is that?' sneered James. 'Thank goodness I've got football practice.'

Tilly stopped crying, waved her wand and turned James's head into a teapot (although it didn't look any different).

I leant forwards to James so I could have a secret whisper.

'James!' I whispered secretly, 'Why do you think they wanted that cake so badly? It's for Flozzy's party. They'll be eating it!'

'Eating the cake?' gasped James. 'But what can I do?'

'Go along with Tilly and help out. You'll be showing Ellie's mum that there's no hard feelings about

169

the competition. You could offer to cut the cake for them,' I said. 'That way you could make sure there's no . . . er . . . *nasty surprises*.'

James's eyes lit up with excitement. He could slip the remote out and chop the rest of the cake into bits and nobody would know!

'Are you talking about my cake?' asked the grumpy man with rainbow toenails. 'What do you mean *nasty surprises*?'

'Don't worry, Dad,' said James. 'I'll get rid of any bits that look funny, even if it means I'm late for football practice.'

'You needn't be too late,' I said. 'You can wear your football kit underneath it, so when you get to the pitch you just have to take it off, and you'll be ready.'

Mum, Dad, James and Tilly all stared at me blankly. They had absolutely no idea what I was talking about ha ha! So I just sat there smiling sweetly at James, and waited for him to ask the question that was bothering them all.

'I don't understand,' said James. 'I can wear my kit underneath *what*? And then take *what* off?'

'Oh honestly James,' I said. 'It's obvious isn't it? You're going to a magic woodland party. There's no way they're going to let you in without . . . *a costume*!'

If You Go Down to the Woods Today . . .

●●●●●●●●●●●●●●●●●●●●●●●●●●●

Here comes the most useful bit of information in this book: happiness is watching your eleven-year-old brother trying to get into a six-year-old's fairy dress.

Oh yes! When Mum had first

mentioned the woodland party, my idea had been that James should wear my old fairy costume. He wasn't happy about it, not happy AT ALL! But by the time the next afternoon had arrived, James had realised that he didn't have much choice.

We all spent about twenty minutes watching him stick his feet through the legholes of the leotard and then roll around the floor as he tried to pull the shoulder straps up.

It was no good, he could only do it if he was bent double, and instead of a fairy he looked like a squashed fly.

Obviously the fairy outfit wasn't going to work, but what else could James use for a woodland party costume? It isn't every day that you get a chance to make your big brother wear absolutely anything you want. I was tugging at my hair like I do when I'm having a think when suddenly: 'I know where there's a costume!' I said. 'In the shed!'

'The shed?' they all gasped.

'There's only a few spades and the hosepipe,' said Dad. 'And that smelly old red armchair.'

'Perfect,' I said. Everybody looked at me like I'd gone bonkers, but I hadn't.

Soon James was standing outside the shed with the big flat cushion from the armchair tied across the top of his head. Mum had brought out an old white sheet and Tilly helped her wrap it all round James's body and fix it with safety pins. It turned out even better than I thought it would! Can you guess what James was supposed to be? I'll give you a clue: what's this book called?

Yes indeed James had turned into the perfect giant mushroom with a white stalk and a red top. What's more, he had to stay that way: '... *or you're not coming to the party!*' said Tilly strictly.

It got even better when Dad tipped the recycling bin out and found a load of round lids from jam jars and pickled onion pots. We got some tape and stuck the lids all over the cushion because it's a fact that magic woodland mushrooms are always spotty. It's true, you ask anyone. By the time we'd finished James looked like a total whoopsie, and the best bit was that the sheet round his legs meant that he could

only move along
by doing little
jumps and
that
made all
the lids come
loose and rattle
about. Was that
wicked or what?
**Ha ha ha
ha ha!**

'Don't you DARE tell my friends about this,' James warned me.

Honestly James! He really shouldn't go giving me ideas. And just then I looked over the fence and spotted Martha staring down at us from her bedroom window. She had a big laugh on her face.

'Don't worry James,' I said to him, but I knew Martha was listening. 'I couldn't tell your friends even if I wanted to. I don't have their phone numbers.'

'Good,' said James.

When I looked back at Martha's window, she was gone. Martha quite likes to kick a football with the boys sometimes, and she DID have their numbers. She knew they wouldn't want to miss this!

'It's time to go,' said Tilly. 'Or we'll be late.'

It took James ages to waddle, hop and shuffle himself in the back door and through to our hallway. Tilly ran ahead and opened the front door. Odd Street was all very quiet so James took a deep breath and then jumped out, hopped down our little front path and on to the pavement. *Ping dang doddle!* went all the lids.

As you should know by now, Ellie Slippin and all her lot are only two doors along at number 9, but James could only do his silly little jumps. It took him ages to get there, with Tilly

the fairy skipping round and round him turning him into a banana, a cheese stick and an umbrella along the way.

'OH WOW OH WOW OH WOW!' came Ivy's voice as we passed number 7. She had seen us out of their downstairs window. 'THAT IS SO . . . OH WOW!'

Ivy was making so much noise that the Slippin front door opened and Ellie came out. She's a bit nervous is Ellie, so as soon as she saw James, she hurried out past their little front flower bed and came to stand behind me for safety.

'I have bad dreams about giant mushrooms,' said Ellie. 'They scare me.'

'Don't worry Ellie, they can't hurt you,' I told her.

'They can when they've got vampire teeth and machine guns,' said Ellie.

Poor Ellie. James must have been the most unscary thing ever, but I

184

could feel her shaking behind me. By this time a whole crowd of pixies, elves, goblins and other fairies had come pouring out of the front door. Flozzy and her friends were all a lot smaller than James, and as soon as they saw him they gathered around to stand under his sofa cushion and do a happy little woodland dance.

'What a lovely costume, James,' said a big jolly gnome who turned out to be Ellie's uncle. 'Let's have a photo of everybody, and I want you in the middle.'

FLASH went the camera. All the little girls rushed over to see themselves on the little screen, leaving James standing awkwardly by the gate.

'Oh James, you were looking down,' said the gnome. 'All we can see is the cushion. We'll have one more, but this time James, let's see your face and give us a big smile. Say cheese.'

All the little girls ran back giggling and hugged James's legs. The big gnome was holding the camera all ready. James was staring at the ground but he knew he was going to have to get this over with.

He took a deep breath then looked up and did a big sunny smile . . .

'*Cheeeeeeeeeese!*'

. . . Just as two boys in football kit rode past on their bikes.

'Hey look, it's JAMES!' screamed Matty the goalkeeper. 'What team do you think YOU'RE on, James?'

'Wait till we tell the others!' cried Liam.

'Wah ha ha ha ha ha ha ha . . . !' They were laughing so much that I

thought they were going to fall off
their bikes.

'Come back here you two!'

screamed James. He tried to run after them. *Ping tinkle dinkle!* went all the lids.

'Oh no!' whimpered Ellie clutching my arm. 'It's a giant mushroom that chases people! I've NEVER been so scared in my WHOLE LIFE!'

But James had forgotten about the sheet round his legs. Hop hop . . . *plop!* James fell over and landed face-first in the flower bed.

By this time the other boys had shot off round the corner but we could still hear them laughing. Meanwhile James was struggling so hard to get up he didn't realise he'd got a flower stuck to his ear. *FLASH* went the camera. 'Sorry,' said the big gnome and all the little girls giggled. 'I couldn't resist it, but at least I got your face that time.'

Even Ellie started to giggle. She went to help him up and said:

'Thank you James. I'll never be scared of mushrooms again.'

'Get off me,' sulked James crossly.

'Be nice,' I said to him. 'And then maybe Ellie can arrange for you to help cut the cake up.'

James suddenly looked hopeful. 'Oh yes! Can I?'

Ellie looked at me as if James had gone potty, so I explained. 'He loves cutting cakes. It really makes his day, especially if you let him do it in private.'

So Ellie and the giant mushroom went inside on a cake-cutting mission, Flozzy and the little people danced around the big jolly gnome and Tilly turned me into an elephant. What a lovely happy ending to the story, don't you think?

Only it isn't the end yet.

Who's Laughing Now?

Later on that night, the front door banged open and James stomped in. I was sitting on the sofa and he just threw his sheet and cushion over me. Oooh temper temper!

194

'Not going to football, James?' asked Dad who was in the armchair watching telly again.

'NO.'

By now I'd got the sheet off and held it up. It was covered in coloured patches of sauce and icing. It looked rather groovy actually.

'What's all that mess?' asked Dad.

'Your cake,' sulked James.

'Oh!' said Dad. 'How was it?'

'Perfect!' said James giving me a

really filthy look. 'Absolutely nothing wrong with it at all.'

'Don't sound so surprised,' said Dad. 'I told you it was one of the all-time greats. Now let's get that sheet into the washing machine.'

The telly clicked off, but there was no one near it. James was astonished until he saw that Dad was holding the TV remote. 'Where did that come from?' he gasped.

'It was in the kitchen all the

time,' said Dad. 'It had fallen inside the oven glove hanging on the back of the door.'

Dad took the sheet through and James stared after him looking confused. His little baked-bean brain was trying to work out how he'd managed to throw the remote round to the other side of the door and into an oven glove that he was sure hadn't even been there before. Ooooh . . . so how DID it get there I wonder? Ha ha! But I had to be careful not to give myself away.

'At least it's turned up,' I said

sounding all cool and casual.

'Why did you tell me it was in the cake?' hissed James.

'Me? I never did,' I said. 'It must have all been in your imagination.'

(Go on, you can turn back and check if you like. I never said anything about it going in the cake until James started it! Ha ha loser.)

'I hate little sisters!' he scowled, and went stomping upstairs to get away from everybody and everything.

It had all been very satisfactory, and what's more, guess what was just about to start on the telly? *Sing, Wiggle and Shine: The Backstage Special*. I got myself nicely laid out on the sofa just as the music was starting. Ahhhh . . . it was well-deserved perfect luxury.

But that's when Tilly came in. She could have sat on the armchair, but she didn't. Instead she pulled my legs off the sofa, and then climbed up and sat herself down right close up next to me.

'This is a bit boring,' said Tilly.

'Then go away,' I told her. 'I'm watching it.'

'I want to watch *Ballet Bears*,' said Tilly.

'No way little girl. I was here first.'

Tilly sat there very quietly for a minute. It was spooky. Tilly never sat that quietly. It was putting me right off. 'Tilly, can't you just go away?' I said.

'But I want to watch *Ballet Bears*.'

'Well you can't.'

'Oh yes I can.' Tilly sounded very sure of herself.

I didn't like the sound of this, especially when she went on to say my name really slowly like this: 'Ag-gath-aaar? You know when James was prodding the cake and the telly channel changed?'

No, I didn't like the sound of this one bit.

'Does James know that you were hiding the remote up your sleeve and pushing the buttons? I know, I saw you. You wouldn't like me to tell him, would you?'

Tilly lay back on the sofa and brought her legs up so she could push me off, but she didn't have to. I know when I'm beaten. All I could do was get up and hand over the remote.

Ballet Bears came on, and Tilly rolled

over to make herself comfortable.

Just for once I found myself

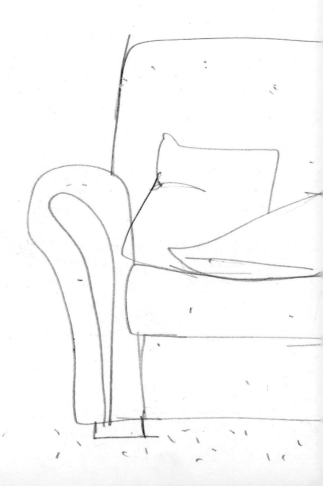

agreeing with James. Gosh I *hate*
little sisters too.

The Ending

● ●

That's the end of the story, and ever since then James has been really nice and we've all lived happily ever after in our little house at number 5 Odd Street . . .

. . . and *that's* a big fat lie ha ha! But you guessed that didn't you? So give yourself a round of applause clap clap clap WAHOO for YOU.

Of course James is still as horrible as ever, but I'll tell you something secretly true about big brothers. If we didn't have any big brothers in the world, it wouldn't be so much fun. For instance, there was one time when James was getting emails from our cousin Bella who we never see, and she ended up thinking he was in big deep LOVE with her! (Gosh how could that have happened eh? OK I admit it was sort of my fault, I had this idea that went just a little bit slightly wrong . . . oooops ha ha!)

Sadly the old bloke that's typing all this out for me says we've nearly run out of pages, so we'll have to leave that story for another book. Instead I'll fill up the last bit of space with a cake recipe which might come in handy for you if your school is having a fete. Hope you like it and **WELL DONE** for reading all of this book because it's got 12,731 words! (The old bloke just counted them on his computer).

And remember, if you **HAVE** got a big brother, don't be too mean to him. He can't help being a) big and b) a brother. What's he supposed to do about it? Turn into a pet rabbit or a giant pizza or something?

Ha ha that'd be so wicked!

Good Byeeeeeeee!

X X X

How to Make a Cake
by Agatha Jane Parrot...

This is how to make a sponge cake. (Other cakes are a bit harder and fruit cakes take ages so it's better to buy one in a shop.)

What you need:

- A cupful of soft butter or margarine (or maybe a bit less)
- A cupful of caster sugar. This is like normal sugar but more powdery.
- A cupful of self-raising flour (or maybe a bit more)
- 3 eggs
- Loads of jam and cream and stuff

What you have to do:

1. Get an old person to turn on the oven so it warms up. Tell them that it needs to be set to 4°C or gas mark 180. Or maybe it's the other way round.

2. Mix up the butter and the caster sugar in a big bowl. You need to squidge it round and round with a spoon so it all turns into a big mushy lump.

3. Break the eggs into a different bowl. Pick all the bits of shell out then whizz them round with a fork until all the yellow and white is mixed up. Don't lick the fork because that's gross.

4. Pour the eggs in with the sugar and butter mush and stir it up so it's slimy and mushy.

5. Sprinkle flour on the top and keep squidging it round all the time until all the flour is mixed in.

6. Put the stuff in a cake tin for cooking but BEFORE YOU DO, you have to rub round the inside of the tin with a bit of butter or it will all stick and burn on the insides.

7. Get your helpful old person to put the tin of mix in the oven. That way if anybody gets a burn on their finger it's them and not you.

8. Go and watch telly for 20 minutes while the old person moans about how messy the kitchen is.

9. Return to find the kitchen is miraculously clean. Ask old person to get cake out of the oven.

10. Go and watch more telly until the cake cools down.

11. Cover cake with cream and jam and stuff while the old person moans about how they only just cleaned the kitchen and now it's even worse than before. And there's your cake. **Ta-dah!**

Serves 6 people. (That's if you cut it into 6 bits. If you cut it into 8 bits then it serves 8 people. And if Martha gets to it first then it only serves 1 person.)

EGMONT PRESS: ETHICAL PUBLISHING

Egmont Press is about turning writers into successful authors and children into passionate readers – producing books that enrich and entertain. As a responsible children's publisher, we go even further, considering the world in which our consumers are growing up.

Safety First
Naturally, all of our books meet legal safety requirements. But we go further than this; every book with play value is tested to the highest standards – if it fails, it's back to the drawing-board.

Made Fairly
We are working to ensure that the workers involved in our supply chain – the people that make our books – are treated with fairness and respect.

Responsible Forestry
We are committed to ensuring all our papers come from environmentally and socially responsible forest sources.

**For more information, please visit our website at
www.egmont.co.uk/ethical**

Egmont is passionate about helping to preserve the world's remaining ancient forests. We only use paper from legal and sustainable forest sources, so we know where every single tree comes from that goes into every paper that makes up every book.

This book is made from paper certified by the Forestry Stewardship Council (FSC®), an organisation dedicated to promoting responsible management of forest resources. For more information on the FSC, please visit **www.fsc.org**. To learn more about Egmont's sustainable paper policy, please visit **www.egmont.co.uk/ethical**.